BALLPARK
Mysteries 7
THE
SAN FRANCISCO
SPLASH

BALLPARK Mysteries 7

THE SAN FRANCISCO SPLASH

by David A. Kelly

illustrated by Mark Meyers

A STEPPING STONE BOOK™
Random House 🏠 New York

*This book is dedicated to all the great children's librarians out there,
who contribute more to kids' learning than anyone will ever know.*
—D.A.K.

For Preston, Angie, Drayk, and Willow
—M.M.

"They throw the ball, I hit it; they hit the ball, I catch it."
—Willie Mays, San Francisco Giants

Text copyright © 2013 by David A. Kelly
Cover art and interior illustrations copyright © 2013 by Mark Meyers

Visit us on the Web!
SteppingStonesBooks.com
randomhouse.com/kids

Educators and librarians, for a variety of teaching tools, visit us at
RHTeachersLibrarians.com

Library of Congress Cataloging-in-Publication Data
Kelly, David A. (David Andrew)
The San Francisco splash / by David A. Kelly ;
illustrated by Mark Meyers. — 1st ed.
p. cm. — (Ballpark mysteries ; #7)
"A Stepping Stone Book."
Summary: "While they are kayaking outside the San Francisco Giants' ballpark, Mike and Kate rescue an old ballplayer who has fallen overboard and discover his World Series ring is missing."—Provided by publisher.
ISBN 978-0-307-97779-3 (pbk.) — ISBN 978-0-307-97780-9 (lib. bdg.) — ISBN 978-0-307-97781-6 (ebook)
[1. Baseball—Fiction. 2. Kayaks and kayaking—Fiction. 3. San Francisco Giants (Baseball team)—Fiction. 4. Mystery and detective stories.] I. Meyers, Mark, ill. II. Title.
PZ7.K2936San 2013 [Fic]—dc23 2012031565

Printed in the United States of America
10 9 8 7 6 5 4 3 2 1

First Edition

Contents

Chapter 1   **A Giant Splash**   1

Chapter 2   **Ray's Ring**   11

Chapter 3   **A Rotten Rival**   18

Chapter 4   **The Thief Confesses**   29

Chapter 5   **Picture This**   42

Chapter 6   **The Proof Is
              in the Picture**   51

Chapter 7   **The Rock**   60

Chapter 8   **A Real Clinker**   74

Chapter 9   **One More Giant Splash**   90

**Dugout Notes ☆
San Francisco Giants Ballpark**   100

A Giant Splash

Kate Hopkins stretched her hand over the edge of her kayak in San Francisco Bay. A white baseball bobbed in the water a couple of feet away. Just a few more inches and she'd have it.

"Are you crazy?" asked her cousin Mike Walsh. He paddled slowly in a nearby kayak. "You might tip over! This water is freezing, even in the summer!"

"I can get it!" Kate said. "Almost there . . ."

Kate's kayak rocked back and forth as she reached. She strained to close her fingers around the floating ball. But each time the ball slipped past and Kate came up empty.

"Geez, *you're* about to fall in, too!" Mike said. "Try this instead."

He paddled his kayak next to Kate's. The noses of their kayaks touched, leaving a bright blue-green triangle of water between them. In the middle of that triangle bobbed the baseball.

Mike nudged the ball with his paddle. It dipped underwater for a moment, but then popped up about a foot closer to Kate. This time she easily plucked the ball from the waves.

"Got it!" Kate called out. She held up the dripping baseball for Mike to see. "Thanks for the assist!"

"No problem, cousin," he said. "That's why they call me Captain Clutch. I get the job done."

"No one calls you that," Kate said. "Besides, the only thing you usually finish is dessert.

Maybe they should call you Captain Cookie instead."

Mike frowned for a moment. Then a smile spread across his freckled face. "That works, too," he said. "I take a *bite* out of the competition!"

Mike turned his kayak to face the stadium. Mike and Kate were in town for a San Francisco Giants game. They were staying in a hotel with Kate's dad.

The stadium loomed over a part of the bay called McCovey Cove, named for a famous Giants player. Beyond the tan wall with rounded arches was the stadium's right field. A walkway stretched along the outside of the stadium.

Since the Giants' stadium was right next to the water, home-run balls sometimes flew over the wall and splashed into the green waves of the bay. They were called splash hits. Lots of boaters and kayakers came early to try to catch a splash hit during batting practice. Kate, Mike, and Kate's dad had rented kayaks earlier that morning.

"Here comes another hit!" Kate's dad called out. He floated in a dark green kayak a few feet away.

The ball sailed high over the right-field wall. Its white leather gleamed in the sun.

Splash!

The ball plopped into the water next to a sailboat about a hundred feet away. Mike and Kate watched two black-and-white curly-haired dogs jump off the boat into the water. They swam to the ball, and one of the dogs grabbed it in its mouth. Then they paddled back to the boat. On the deck again, the dogs shook off while a tall man in an orange-and-black jersey held up the ball.

"Boy, you have to be fast," Kate's dad said. "Maybe we should wait out here until the game and see if my Dodgers can light up San Francisco's pitchers. I'm sure there'll be lots of splash hits!"

Kate's dad worked as a scout for the Los Angeles Dodgers. The Dodgers were in town to play a weekend series against the Giants. The Dodgers and the Giants had been fierce rivals for over 125 years. Both teams had moved to California from New York City in 1958.

"You think the Dodgers will win today?" Kate asked. She loved baseball, too.

"They have a good chance," her dad said. "But I have to admit, the Giants are a pretty good team. Being such strong rivals is what makes these games so great."

"Well, I'm rooting for the San Francisco Giants," Mike called out from his kayak. "They're the hometown team!"

"And I'm rooting for the Dodgers, since they're my dad's team!" Kate said.

Mike paddled backward and forward, waiting for a chance at another ball. He kept one eye on the stadium and one eye on the other boaters. He was determined to beat them to the next splash hit.

Suddenly, Kate pointed toward the park. "There's one!" she cried. "And it's coming this way!"

The ball flew long and straight. It seemed more like a line drive than a big pop fly. It headed right toward them.

Mike was ready. He reached up as high as he could while still sitting in the kayak. He cupped his hands just as the ball came close.

Swish!

The ball flew past Mike, a few feet above his head. It landed with a plop about twenty feet behind him. A man in a silver kayak fished it out of the water with a net.

"Drat!" Mike exclaimed. "This is hard. Why can't I get one?"

Mike, Kate, and Kate's dad went back to scanning the sky for more hits. The minutes ticked by, but no balls flew their way. Mike paddled in circles, waiting.

KERSPLASH!

Something dropped into the water nearby.

"What was that?" Kate's dad asked.

Kate gasped. She pointed to the large motorboat next to them.

"Man overboard!" Kate yelled.

Mike saw a man with gray hair thrashing
in the water. The man was trying to grab hold
of the side of the white motorboat.

"I'm on it!" Mike cried. He dug his paddle

into the water as if he was crushing home runs at the batting cage. His kayak shot over to the man floundering in the bay.

Mike stowed the paddle in his kayak. He pulled his knees up to his chest, even though it was awkward with his life jacket on.

"I'll save him!" he shouted.

Without another thought, Mike jumped into the water!

Ray's Ring

"Arrrgh!" Mike screamed, his teeth chattering. "This water is *freezing*!"

"Mike! Come back!" Kate shouted. "You're crazy!"

But Mike didn't listen. Nearby, the older man still struggled to get into the boat. Each time the captain of the motorboat came close to pulling him up, the man slipped back into the water. There was no one else on the boat to offer help.

Mike swam over. He grabbed the man's Giants warm-up jacket from behind.

"Don't worry," Mike said. "I'll help you get out. Next time the captain pulls, I'll push!"

The captain took the older man's hand. While he pulled, Mike shoved hard, kicking fast to stay above the water. This time, the older man hoisted himself over the side and slumped onto the deck of the boat.

All around them, the other kayakers and boaters clapped.

Mike treaded water. The captain of the boat threw a heavy blanket around the man and checked him over.

"He's going to be fine," the captain said as he stood up. "He just needs to dry off. Here, let me give you a hand, son."

The captain pulled on Mike's life jacket as Mike clawed his way over the side. His feet dropped to the deck, and he leaned against the edge of the boat, panting.

"That was harder than I thought," Mike said.

"It was a brave thing you did," the captain said. He wrapped a gray blanket around Mike. "Most people don't want to go swimming in San Francisco Bay! By the way, I'm Captain Dan."

"I'm Mike. I'm with them," Mike said as Kate and her father pulled up alongside the motorboat in their kayaks. "That's Kate and my uncle Steve."

Mike's empty kayak floated between them. Captain Dan helped them aboard the boat. Then he tied their kayaks to the back railing.

"What happened?" Kate asked.

The older man pointed to the low side of the boat. "I always wanted to come out in the bay to try to catch a splash hit," he said. "I was standing right there, watching for balls, when I felt something bump my back. The next thing I knew, I was in the water!"

Captain Dan stepped forward. "That's right," he said. "I was trying to keep the boat steady when I saw a big wave coming. I turned to grab him, but I couldn't get a good hold on his jacket. Then the wave rocked the boat and he fell in."

Huddled in the blanket, the man looked at his dripping-wet feet. "I guess I'm not Ray the Rock anymore," he said. "It used to be that nothing could knock me off my game."

"Holy cow! You're Ray Reynolds?" Kate's dad asked.

"Sure am," Ray replied. "Been him all my life!"

"Kids, this is all-star pitcher Ray Reynolds, from one of the most famous Giants World Series teams ever," Kate's dad explained. "He was the pitcher the Dodgers never, ever wanted to face."

"Nice to meet you, Mr. Reynolds," Mike and Kate said at the same time.

"Please, call me Ray," Ray Reynolds said.

"So what are you doing here?" Kate's dad asked.

Ray shook his head. "I'm in town for this weekend's games," he said. "We're reliving the

historic back-to-back World Series wins of the
Dodgers and the Giants—"

"Wait, the Giants played the Dodgers in
the World Series two years in a row?" Mike
interrupted.

Ray laughed. "No. They both played other
teams. But they won the World Series one after

the other. The Giants won the first year, and the Dodgers won the second year. My old rival Lenny Littleton is throwing out the first pitch today for the Dodgers. I'm doing the same thing tomorrow for the Giants."

Ray pulled himself upright. The blanket slipped off his shoulders. He glanced at the outline of the Giants' stadium and went into a pitcher's position. He started to pretend to throw a ball toward home plate, but he stopped in the middle of the delivery. He held up his right hand with a puzzled look on his face.

"Oh no!" he cried. "My World Series ring is missing!"

A Rotten Rival

Ray's long fingers stretched out in the sun. Mike and Kate could see a tan line where the ring used to be.

"I put the ring on this morning," Ray said. "It's from the year we won the World Series. It's gold with a big ruby in the middle."

"Maybe it fell off on the boat," Kate said.

Mike and Kate scrambled around the motorboat looking for the ring. Captain Dan searched in the front, while Mike, Kate, and Kate's dad looked on the sides and in the back.

Ray checked his pockets. No one found the missing ring.

"Nada," Kate said. "Nothing." Kate was teaching herself Spanish. She liked to try out new words when she had a chance.

Captain Dan let out a long sigh. "It's definitely *not* here," he said. "I'm sorry, Ray, but we've looked everywhere. I think the ring must have been missing before you got on the boat."

Kate eyed the green waves of the bay. She dipped her hand into the frigid water. "What if it fell off in the water?" she asked. "It's so cold it might have slipped off Ray's finger and dropped to the bottom of the bay!"

"Wow, you're right! That's what must have happened," Captain Dan said. He checked the boat's instruments. "I'll write down exactly where we were when Ray fell overboard. Maybe a diver can come back and search for the ring."

Ray studied his hand. "I'm pretty sure it didn't fall off in the water," he said.

Captain Dan handed Ray a slip of yellow paper. "Here's our exact location," he said. "You can use that to have a diver search. For now, let's get back to shore to warm up."

He pointed the boat toward the ballpark and pulled up to the walkway in front of the stadium. Mike and Kate hopped onto shore and slipped off their life jackets. Mike huddled in his blanket, running in place to keep warm.

As Mr. Hopkins tied the kayaks to the dock, Kate pulled a waterproof plastic bag from the pocket of her jacket. She unzipped it, took out two cell phones, and handed one to Mike.

"I've got to get back to Fisherman's Wharf to pick up another passenger," Captain Dan said, checking his watch. "You can leave the blankets with the Giants' front office. I'll get them later."

While Kate watched the motorboat pull away, Mike punched a few search words into his phone. He held up the phone for Kate, Mr. Hopkins, and Ray to see.

On the screen was a picture of a heavy gold ring with WORLD CHAMPIONS spelled out on the top and bottom. In the center was a diamond shaped like a baseball infield.

Ray smiled. "That's the ring!" he said. "Except mine has a big red stone in the middle. They made it special for me, since I had an important play in a big game." His smile turned into a frown. "I've just got to get it back somehow."

Under his blanket, Mike began to shiver again.

"We need to change into warmer clothes

first," Ray said, heading toward the stadium entrance. "I bet we can find something in the locker room."

After they passed through the gates, Mr. Hopkins told Kate and Mike he had to go to the visiting dugout to get ready for the game. Mike and Kate waved goodbye and followed Ray through some large hallways to the Giants' locker room. On the way, they passed loads of fans coming into the park. Most wore the black-and-orange colors of the Giants. But a lot had on the Dodgers' blue and white.

Outside the clubhouse door, Ray talked to a security guard, who waved them inside.

"Hey, Mickey!" Ray called to a middle-aged man standing near the dugout entrance. He wore a Giants T-shirt. "Mike and I took a little swim in the bay. Do you think you can find us some dry clothes?"

"No problem, Ray," Mickey said. Mike guessed that Mickey was a clubhouse attendant for the Giants. "Anything for an all-star like you!"

Kate sat down on a bench in the middle of the room while Mickey checked a supply closet. He grabbed some clean clothes and led Mike and Ray into a nearby changing room.

They returned a few minutes later, all decked out. Ray had changed into an old-fashioned Giants uniform, while Mike wore a team jersey, orange sweatpants, and a new pair of Giants sandals.

"Wow! I'd never guess which team you're rooting for today," Kate said.

"Thanks," Mike said, taking a seat beside Kate. "I said we should root for the hometown team."

Ray slumped down and looked at his empty

ring finger. "It just doesn't feel the same without my ring." He sighed.

Kate twirled her long brown ponytail
around her finger. "Are you sure you had it on
this morning?" she asked.

Ray raised his eyebrows. "That's it!" he

said. "In all the excitement, I forgot about this morning. I'll bet I wasn't even wearing the ring by the time I took the boat ride!"

Mike's and Kate's jaws dropped. "What do you mean?" Kate asked.

Ray punched his fist into his palm. "I know who took the ring," he said. "Lenny Littleton! He was my biggest rival on the Dodgers!"

Ray went on to explain that just before the boat ride, he'd been signing autographs with Lenny outside the stadium.

"Lenny *always* gives me a hard time. He thinks we stole a season-ending win from the Dodgers because of an important play that I made," Ray said. "He's been mad at me ever since!"

Ray explained that after they had signed autographs that morning, Lenny had challenged Ray to an arm-wrestling match.

"It was right before I got on Captain Dan's boat," Ray said. "But first, Lenny had us each take off our World Series rings. We put them to the side of the table."

"Who won?" Mike asked.

"I did!" Ray said, puffing out his chest. "I always beat him fair and square, even if he doesn't like it."

"He probably scooped up your ring when you won," Kate said. "Tricky!"

Ray told them how after he and Lenny had finished arm wrestling, a photographer had taken pictures of them with fans. Then Ray had boarded Captain Dan's boat to look for splash hits.

"I guess I was so excited about winning that I forgot to put my ring back on," Ray said. "Let's go track Lenny down and get it back."

As they headed for the door, Mickey called

out to Ray, "Don't forget you're the guest of honor for that charity event upstairs. You're going to be late unless you hurry!"

Ray stopped. "Oh no," he said. "I can't miss that event."

"Don't worry, Ray," Kate said. "Mike and I will go talk to Lenny. We'll get your ring back!"

The Thief Confesses

"My dad's in the Dodgers' dugout," Kate said. "I bet Lenny is there, too."

After saying goodbye to Ray, Mike and Kate started down the hallway toward the out-field. But Mike stopped abruptly. "Hey, Kate," he said. "Wait a minute."

Kate wheeled around to see Mike dart across the hallway to a souvenir booth. Giants T-shirts sat stacked on the sides. Fluffy white-and-black wool hats that looked like panda heads dangled from the ceiling.

By the time Kate caught up, the salesperson had put out a series of colorful bracelets on the counter. They came in three colors—orange, black, and white, as well as an orange-and-black-striped version. Kate picked one up.

"These are MightiBands," the salesperson explained to Mike and Kate. "They have a special magnetic core that gives your wrist extra power for hitting."

Mike fiddled with an orange one. He popped it over his right hand onto his wrist. It was snug, but not too tight.

"I feel stronger already," Mike said. He turned to Kate. "Here, try to turn my hand upside down."

Kate rolled her eyes. She grabbed Mike's hand and twisted. He struggled to keep it steady. Just as Kate was about to flip it over, Mike pulled away.

"Now try the other one, without the MightiBand," he said.

Kate took his other hand. This time, she easily flipped it upside down. It seemed like Mike wasn't even trying to stop her.

"See how powerful it is?" Mike asked. "You couldn't move the hand with the MightiBand."

"I was just about to flip your hand when you switched," Kate said. "And you weren't even trying the second time."

"I don't know about that." Mike pulled the MightiBand off, took out some money, and plunked it on the counter. "I'll take it," he said.

After Mike and Kate left the booth, they followed the walkway behind left field. On their left was a huge, curvy soda bottle, about eighty feet long. Next to it was a gigantic four-fingered baseball glove.

"Wow, cool!" Mike exclaimed. "What are those?"

"If you'd read about the ballpark in the guidebook, you'd know," Kate said. "The giant soda bottle has slides inside." She pointed to a gated area. "You climb up those stairs to the top of the bottle. Then you slide down to the bottom!"

"What's the glove do?" Mike asked.

Kate shrugged. "Nothing. It just looks cool."

"What are we waiting for? Let's try the slides," Mike said.

Kate stopped him. "Not now. We have to see if Lenny has the ring, remember?" She pulled Mike along. "We can come back later. . . ."

As they walked around the outfield, Mike kept holding up the MightiBand on his right hand. "This is great!" he said. "I can't wait to get up to bat."

On the other side of the scoreboard, near center field, they passed a bunch of fans sitting in an old cable car that was behind the center-field seats.

"I don't get how cable cars work," Mike said.

"It's simple," Kate said. "I read about them in

the guidebook. Cable cars are pulled along by a heavy steel cable that runs under the streets. San Francisco is so hilly, something was needed to help people move around the city."

"That's cool!" Mike said as they started down the walkway again. "Maybe we can come back and check that out later, too."

McCovey Cove with its kayakers was on the left. For a moment, Mike and Kate watched the boaters. Then they kept walking until they came to the Dodgers' dugout.

"We're here to see my father," Kate told a security guard near the gate to the visitors' dugout. "That's him over there. Hi, Dad!"

Kate's father waved back from the other side. He spoke to the security guard, who then opened the gate. Mike and Kate slipped into the dugout. A bunch of baseball players stood at the far end. The game was about to start.

Mike took in all the sights. "Wow!" he said. "It's like you're right in the game!"

Kate told her dad all about Ray's arm-wrestling match. "We want to ask Lenny Littleton about the ring," she said.

Kate's dad pointed to a stocky older man

sitting at the other end of the bench. "That's Mr. Littleton," he said. "I know he doesn't care for the San Francisco Giants, but I doubt he'd ever steal Ray's World Series ring."

"Can we go ask, Uncle Steve?" Mike said.

Kate's dad laughed. "No, I don't want you bothering him," he said. "But you can ask him if he comes down this way. And, Mike, you might want to be careful in those clothes!"

Mike leaned against the wall and blushed. His black-and-orange Giants jersey certainly didn't fit in very well in the Dodgers' dugout.

The game started a few minutes later. As Mike and Kate settled back on the bench, Mike drew some funny looks from the Dodgers. He tried to ignore them, but it was hard. Finally, Mike slipped the shirt off. He turned it inside out and put it back on. Now it just looked like a poorly made jersey.

"I wondered how long that would take you," Kate said. Mike felt better right away. He could focus on the game again. As they were watching, he fished a worn green tennis ball out of his sweatpants pocket and rolled it from hand to hand. Mike always carried a ball with him. It helped him think.

The first two innings went by quickly. Neither team scored, but the Giants got close once, with three runners on base.

Partway through the third inning, the Giants got runners on first and third with only one out.

The Los Angeles Dodgers pitcher shook off one sign after the other. He waited for his catcher to select the pitch he wanted. At last, he got the sign he was looking for and went into set position.

It seemed like he was trying to throw a

curveball. But the pitch headed straight for the middle of the plate.

The Giants batter leaned back and unwound on it.

POW!

The ball sailed high over the head of the shortstop and the left fielder. It *plonk*ed into the top of the soda bottle slide. It was a home run!

One runner after the other scored. Now San Francisco was up 3–0.

Mike and Kate were so busy watching the game, they didn't notice that Lenny had gotten up to stretch his legs. He stopped in front of Mike and pointed to Mike's Giants sweatpants and inside-out jersey.

"You sure you're in the right dugout, son?" he asked in a deep, gravelly voice.

"Um—um, yeah," Mike stammered. He looked at Kate for help.

Kate stood up. "Are you Mr. Littleton?" she asked.

"I am," replied the man, bowing slightly. "Lenny Littleton, at your service!"

"I'm Kate," said Kate, "and this is my cousin Mike. We heard you had a World Series ring. May we see it?"

Lenny laughed softly. "Sure," he said. "I'm always happy to show off my ring."

He held out his right hand. On one finger was a huge silver ring. The word DODGERS was set in heavy letters above an oval design. The center of the ring had a gold baseball infield with a small round diamond in the middle.

"Each year they come up with a new design for the World Series rings," Lenny explained. "So they're all different."

"We saw a picture of the one from when the Giants won the Series," Mike said.

Lenny shook his head. "They didn't deserve to win that year," he said. "They beat us to end our season with a sneaky play. I always give my old Giants buddy Ray a hassle about that."

"We just met Ray," Kate said. "Did you know his World Series ring is missing?"

Mike stepped forward, edging Kate aside. "Yeah, Ray thinks you might have taken it!" he said. "Right after he beat you in the arm-wrestling match."

Lenny's eyes grew wide. A sly smile flashed across his face. "That's it," he said. "Ray never deserved that ring. I admit it. I stole Ray's ring!"

"You did?" Mike asked. "Where is it?"

Lenny leaned back and made a pitching motion. "Yeah!" he said. "I stole it and threw it into the bay!"

Picture This

Mike and Kate gasped. "You stole the ring?" Kate asked. "And threw it in the water?"

Lenny laughed out loud.

"I knew Ray didn't trust me," he said. "But I never thought he'd call me a thief!"

Mike folded his arms in front of his chest. "Why'd you steal the ring?" he asked.

"Like I said, he didn't deserve it," Lenny said. "It wasn't fair that the Giants beat us in that game." Lenny examined his ring for a moment, then looked up. "But I'm afraid I'm just pulling your leg, kids. I didn't steal Ray's ring."

"Ray says you asked him to take it off to arm-wrestle," Kate said. "He thinks you scooped it up after that."

Lenny scratched his chin. "No, that's not what happened. We both put our rings back on after we finished arm wrestling. Ray probably doesn't remember. He was busy giving high fives to all the fans because he won. He slipped the ring on without thinking."

"So who took it?" Mike asked.

"I'm not sure," Lenny said. "But it definitely happened *after* we finished with the arm-wrestling match."

Mike scuffed at the ground with his sneaker. "Shoot," he said. "Ray really wants his ring back. Now we don't have any good ideas of where it is."

"World Series rings are worth a lot of

money," Lenny said. "It's possible someone took it to sell it to a collector."

Kate sighed. "But who?" she asked.

Lenny tipped his cap to them. "I'll keep

thinking about it," he said. "I don't like the Giants, but I hope you find Ray's ring. World Series rings are important to us old ballplayers!"

Lenny shuffled back to the end of the dugout. Mike and Kate sat down on the bench again. Kate was deep in thought. Then she turned to Mike.

"Do you believe him?" she whispered. "What if he was lying to us and he really took the ring?"

Mike shook his head. "No, when Lenny talked about the ring, it seemed like he was telling the truth. What are we going to tell Ray?" he said.

Kate leaned back. "I guess you're right. We're stuck," she said finally. "There's no way to prove whether or not Lenny took the ring."

She twirled the end of her ponytail around

her fingers. Mike watched the Giants take the field for the fifth inning.

Kate stood up. "Let's go for a walk and explore," she said. "We're not going to figure it out sitting here."

Mike pulled himself up. "Good idea," he said. "I *am* getting a little hungry. Maybe we can find some food."

"I'm pretty sure we can find food, even if we can't find the ring," Kate said.

They said goodbye to Kate's father and left the dugout.

"Hey, I know," Mike said as they walked up the aisle. "Let's check out that cable car in center field."

On the way toward the outfield, Kate and Mike stopped so Mike could buy a hot dog and some of the Giants' special garlic fries. Kate got a slice of pizza and chips. They walked along, enjoying their snacks and watching the game.

After they passed McCovey Cove, they spotted the cable car behind the center-field seats. Mike broke into a sprint. The cable car looked like a small train car with open sides in the front half. Long benches ran toward the back. There were steps below the benches, and wooden poles for the riders to hang on to.

The words SAN FRANCISCO MUNICIPAL RAILWAY were stenciled on the side of the car. Above the words, the number 44 stood out in bright gold paint.

Mike scrambled up the single step to the platform at the back of the cable car. He ducked inside as Kate followed.

Ring! Ring! Ring! Ring!

Mike pulled the rope cord that hung from the ceiling. It connected to a small brass bell

47

at the front of the car. Its bright sound echoed through the car.

Kate covered her ears. "Yikes! Give it a break," she said. "It's not like we're going to hit anybody!"

They watched the game for a while from the front of the cable car.

At the end of the inning, a Giants' fan photographer walked over with a camera. Mike and Kate scrunched together while the photographer took their picture.

"Perfect!" the woman said. "If you want to see the picture, go to the fan photo booth near the food court in a few minutes. The camera uploads the pictures to a big display with all the fan photos from today."

The photographer waved goodbye and moved on to another group of fans.

Kate punched Mike in the arm.

"Hey, what'd you do that for?" Mike asked, grabbing his arm.

"Don't you see?" she said. "We can't *prove* that Lenny took the ring. But I just thought of a way we might prove that he *didn't* steal it!"

The Proof Is in the Picture

Mike and Kate raced through the stadium, dodging fans carrying hot dogs and garlic fries.

Kate skidded to a halt in front of a big circular stand. A bank of computers flashed pictures of fans taken from around the ballpark.

"Remember, Ray said he signed autographs with Lenny and *then* a photographer took pictures of him with fans," Kate said. "That was right before the boat ride. I'll bet those pictures are here."

Kate swiped her finger across the touch screen to bring up photos from earlier in the day. A picture of Ray and Lenny flickered up on the screen. They were signing autographs at a table near McCovey Cove.

Kate dragged her hand to the right and brought up a picture from a little while later.

"That's it!" she said, stabbing the screen with her finger.

Mike leaned over to look at the picture. It showed Ray standing in front of Captain Dan's boat with his arms around some fans.

"That was before the boat ride," Kate said. "Look closely at this picture."

Mike shrugged. He didn't see anything special. "So? It's a picture of Ray with fans," he said.

"Check out his right hand," Kate said. She pushed the magnifying glass icon on the screen to zoom in.

Mike studied Ray's hand. It was draped over a fan's shoulder. The shiny World Series ring on his finger showed clearly.

"Ah! I get it! That proves that Ray still had the ring when he went for the boat ride," Mike said.

"And there's the boat in the background," Kate added. "He put the ring on after the wrestling match, just like Lenny said."

"That means Ray lost the ring during the ride," Mike said. "It also means that Lenny definitely isn't the thief."

"The ring must have come off when he fell out of the boat," Kate said. She kicked at the ground. "He'll have to get a diver to look for it. But it may be impossible to find down there."

Mike nodded. "Yeah, you're probably right," he said. He leaned against the booth and looked out at the game. It was the eighth inning. The Giants were winning. But Mike didn't feel like celebrating.

The crowd roared as the Giants got the third out and hustled off the field to bat.

Kate nudged Mike. She pointed to the gigantic soda bottle on the left-field wall. "The game's almost over," she said. "Let's take a couple of rides on the slide before we have to tell Ray about the ring."

Mike and Kate climbed the stairs of the giant soda bottle slide and took a moment to look around at the top. Behind them was McCovey Cove. Below them, the Giants were batting.

Kate took a deep breath and plunged down the slide. Mike grabbed the bar over the slide's round entrance hole.

"Watch out below!" he said when the attendant said it was okay to go. Mike flung his body feetfirst into the tunnel. "Wow-oh-wowwee!" he called out on the way down, his voice wavering as he bumped one way and then the other against the sides of the curvy slide.

"Whoa!" Mike gasped as he slid to a stop at the bottom of the slide. Instead of getting up, he leaned back and looked up at the frame of the soda bottle. "That was even better than hitting a home run in Little League!"

"It sure was *rápido*!" Kate added, trying out

more Spanish. "You know, fast! But come on, you've got to get out of the way!"

But Mike didn't budge. He lost himself

listening to the sounds of the baseball game in the background.

Finally, Kate grabbed Mike's hand and tugged. Mike pulled back, but Kate was strong. She grabbed with both hands and struggled to haul Mike to his feet when suddenly his MightiBand popped off in her hands. Mike dropped back onto the slide.

"Aha!" Kate called. She dangled the orange MightiBand in front of Mike. "You want it back? Then get up!"

Mike stood up in a flash. "That's it!" he said.

"I know," Kate said. "See? It worked!"

"No, that's the answer to the missing ring mystery!" Mike said. "I know where the ring went!"

Kate's eyes grew wide. "Where?"

Mike smiled. "Give me the MightiBand, and I'll tell you," he said.

Kate passed the bracelet back, and Mike slipped it on. "I don't think Ray's ring is at the bottom of the bay," he said.

"Where is it, then?" asked Kate.

"It's in Captain Dan's pocket," Mike said. "I'll bet Captain Dan stole the ring when he helped Ray out of the water, just like you pulled the MightiBand off my hand. Captain Dan pushed Ray into the water so he could have a chance to save him. When he helped Ray out of the water, he slipped the ring off Ray's finger. Ray was too cold and scared to notice!"

Kate gave Mike a high five. "I think you're right!" she said. "But if that's the case, we need to catch him before he does something with the ring."

"How are we going to do that?" Mike asked. "We don't know where he is."

Kate bit her lip and thought for a moment.

"Yes, we do! When Captain Dan dropped us off on the walkway, he said he was going back to Fisherman's Wharf," she said. "I'll bet that's where he keeps his boat."

"But how are we going to find his boat?" Mike asked. "All we know is his name. And what if Captain Dan isn't even his real name?"

"I got a good look at the boat after he dropped us off," Kate said. "I saw the name of it, too, but I can't remember what it was."

Mike snapped his fingers. "I saw the last part of the name in a picture at the booth!" he said. "It said *'atch.'* It's probably something like *Fast Match*. If we figure it out, we can ask someone at Fisherman's Wharf."

"It's too late today," Kate said. "But we're sightseeing tomorrow morning with my dad. Fisherman's Wharf can be our first stop. That way, we can go fishing for a thief!"

59

The Rock

The next morning, Mike, Kate, and Kate's dad boarded a cable car in Union Square for Fisherman's Wharf. Along the way, Mike and Kate brainstormed ideas for finding Captain Dan's boat.

"It will be easier if we can figure out the boat's name," Kate said. "We know it ends in *'atch.'*"

"Was it *Door Latch* or *Itchy Scratch*?" Mike asked.

"Nah. I think it's something like *Good*

Match," Kate said. "But it could be *Vegetable Patch!*"

The cable car climbed up one of San Francisco's steep hills. Kate's father sat on a wooden bench, facing outward. Mike and Kate stood on the steps and hung on to the poles. The cable car kept stopping to pick up people or to wait at red lights. Mike and Kate had to be extra-careful they weren't leaning out too far when another cable car went by in the other direction, or they might get hit!

"Psst, Kate. Look at that man's ring," Mike whispered. He pointed to a man who had just sat down next to Kate's dad.

Kate glanced at the man. He was middle-aged and wearing a huge gold ring on his right hand.

Kate's eyes grew wide. "That looks like a World Series ring," she whispered back.

"I know," Mike said. "What if he's the thief and it's Ray's ring?"

Kate stared at the ring. She couldn't tell. "We've got to do something soon," she said. "We're getting close to the end of the ride."

Mike edged around Kate so he was standing in front of the man. He cleared his throat. The man looked up from his phone.

Mike pointed at the man's hand. "Is that a World Series ring?" he asked. "It looks really cool."

"It sure is," the man said. He held out his hand so Mike and Kate had a better view. The ring looked just like the picture that Mike had pulled up on his phone the day before. Mike glanced at Kate and shook his head. The center of the ring had a big shiny diamond, not a ruby. It wasn't Ray's ring.

"My father was on an old Giants team that

won the World Series," the man said. "He gave it to me to wear. He played with all the great players. He even played with Willie Mays."

"Oh wow," Kate said. "I love Willie Mays. He was one of the best players of all time. He made that incredible over-the-shoulder catch in the World Series."

The cable car jerked to a halt. "Everyone out!" called the conductor. People jumped off the car onto the street.

The man with the ring stood up. "Willie Mays *was* amazing," he said. "If I only had a ball, I could show you what that catch looked like."

Mike smiled. He pulled the tennis ball out of his pants pocket.

"Perfect! Throw me a high one," the man said. He jumped off the cable car and ran up the street.

Mr. Hopkins and Kate watched as Mike

tossed the ball high into the air. The tennis ball
arched over a small tree. The man, still running away, held his hands up in front of him.

The ball plopped over his left shoulder, into his upstretched hands!

Kate, Mike, and Mr. Hopkins clapped. The man turned around to give them a thumbs-up.

"I'm not Willie Mays, but that wasn't a bad basket catch!" the man said. He tossed the ball back to Mike, waved, and walked away.

Kate gasped. "Basket catch!" she said.

Mike nodded. "Yes, Kate," he said. "That's what he just did."

Kate rolled her eyes. "No, you dope!" she said. "It's also the name of the boat—*Basket Catch*!"

Mike gave Kate a fist bump. "That's it!" he said. "Good work."

Mike, Kate, and Mr. Hopkins wandered through the tourist area of Fisherman's Wharf, which was filled with gift shops and tour buses. In the background, the bright orange Golden

Gate Bridge stretched across San Francisco Bay.

"I bet Captain Dan's boat is over there by the water," Kate said to her dad. "Can we go see?"

"Sure, let's meet back here in fifteen minutes," Mr. Hopkins said. "I want to take some pictures of these colorful shops."

Mike and Kate crossed the street and rounded the corner of a big brick building. On the other side was the harbor with a long set of piers lined with boats. "Perfect!" Mike said. "Let's start looking, cuz."

Mike and Kate went up and down each dock, looking for Captain Dan's boat. Finally, Kate spotted it. Red letters on the stern spelled out *Basket Catch*. Mike and Kate ran over to it. The boat was empty.

"Now what?" Mike asked. "Captain Dan isn't here. We can't ask him about the ring."

Kate looked around. No one was close by. "Give me your ball," she said.

"What?" Mike asked.

"The tennis ball! Quick, throw me your tennis ball," Kate said.

Mike pulled the tennis ball out of his sweatshirt pocket and tossed it to Kate. But instead of catching it, she ducked. The ball sailed over her head.

BWOP! BOING! BWOP!

It landed in the middle of Captain Dan's boat! The ball bounced to a stop against the seats.

"Oh well." Kate shrugged. "I guess I have to go get it!"

Kate hopped over the railing. She quickly lifted up the life jackets and the edges of the seats, checking all the nooks. Finally, she spotted a piece of paper wedged into a small space beneath the windshield. She pulled it out.

"Take a look at this," Kate called.

She held up the yellow paper. It read *The rock. The ring. 3pm. Cash.*

"Captain Dan must be meeting someone at three o'clock to sell Ray's ring for cash!" Kate said.

Mike looked at his phone. "It's noon now," he said. "We've got time to look a little bit more, as long as Captain Dan doesn't come back."

Mike and Kate checked the rest of the boat for more clues. But nothing else turned up. They stepped back onto the dock.

"The Rock could mean Ray," Kate said. "Or it could be where they are meeting!"

"Well, there's a rock," Mike said. He pointed to a small divider in the street. A granite boulder stood next to a flagpole.

"I don't know," Kate said. "That doesn't seem like a very good meeting place. Let's keep looking."

They scanned the area for other rocks. But there weren't many. There were plenty of boats, shops, tour buses, and even shrubs. But not a lot of rocks.

Mike bounced his tennis ball on the ground. "This is crazy," he said. "We could be looking for days."

"You're right," Kate said. "But I've got an idea."

Mike followed Kate over to a small white tourist stand near the shops. Kate waited in line until it was her turn to talk to the woman at the window.

"We're supposed to meet our friend," Kate said. "He told us to meet him at a rock around here, but we can't figure out what he meant. Do you know of any rocks that would make good meeting points?"

The woman squinted at Kate. "I guess it's your first trip to San Francisco," she said. The woman stepped out the side door of the stand. She pointed to a small island in the middle of San Francisco Bay. Sunlight gleamed off the windows of an old concrete building.

"If you're looking for the rock, it's right there," she said.

Mike and Kate studied her face to see if she was joking. She wasn't.

"There's a famous old prison on Alcatraz Island," the woman went on. "And a lot of

people call the island the Rock. If you're meeting someone at the Rock, you need to go to Alcatraz!"

Mike and Kate exchanged glances.

"You know what this means, Kate," Mike said. "We're going to prison!"

A Real Clinker

The woman from the tourist stand explained to Kate and Mike that Alcatraz used to be a military base and then a prison. The prison closed in 1963 because it cost too much to run.

"Only the worst criminals were sent there," the woman said. "Al Capone, George 'Machine Gun' Kelly, Alvin 'Creepy' Karpis, and lots of others."

A big stretch of water sat between the prison island and the shore. Mike knew from yesterday how cold the water was. He shuddered.

"Did anyone ever get away?" he asked.

"Thirty-four people tried to escape. Officials said no one ever did," the woman said. Then she leaned over and whispered, "But three prisoners broke out in June 1962. They put fake heads in their beds. Then they escaped through holes they had tunneled into the wall with spoons. They were never found. Many people think they died escaping, but I think they made it to Mexico!"

The woman went on to tell them they could go on a tour of Alcatraz by taking a boat to the island.

Mr. Hopkins was snapping pictures of a huge group of sea lions on the other side of Fisherman's Wharf. The sea lions were trying to sun themselves on a series of wooden docks in the bay. But the sun wasn't cooperating. The day had turned from bright and sunny to chilly and cloudy. Every few seconds, the sea lions made playful barking sounds or mournful growls.

Kate shivered in her sweatshirt. She hugged her dad to warm up. Then she asked him if they could visit Alcatraz.

"Great idea!" Kate's dad said. "I think I've taken enough pictures here." He bought three tickets to the island.

The tour left at one-thirty, and Mike, Kate, and Mr. Hopkins cruised across the bay in a large tour boat. The looming gray prison buildings drew closer. The city wasn't far away, but it was definitely out of reach. Seagulls swooped and screamed overhead as the boat pulled up to the dock.

After Mike, Kate, and Mr. Hopkins stepped off the boat, a park ranger gave the tour group an overview of the island's history. The whole time, Kate kept fidgeting. Dried leaves skittered

by in the wind. It was getting closer and closer
to three o'clock.

"Finally!" she exhaled as the group climbed
a hill to the first building. Dark trees towered
on their left. At the top of the twisty road was
the main prison building. A huge rusty water
tower stood guard on the right. Little sprouts of

pink flowers bloomed against the rocky island scrub.

"Here comes the fog!" Mr. Hopkins said. Wisps of white clouds rolled in from the bay. The fog crept down the embankments and made it hard to see very far. "It's a good thing we didn't come to take pictures of the view!"

"What view?" Mike asked.

Once inside, they walked up a set of metal stairs. Rows of jail cells spread out before them. Grimy orange paint flaked off rusted spots on the thick metal bars.

Mike, Kate, and Mr. Hopkins wandered from one area to another, walking to the different cells and rooms. Mike and Kate kept an eye out for Captain Dan. Most of the cells were empty, except for chipped toilets and small sinks. Some had a bed that hung from the wall on a chain.

Around the corner was a different set of cells with big black steel doors. "Those must be the isolation cells," Kate's dad said. "That's where the really bad criminals were kept."

Tourists crowded in and out of cells, reading the plaques on the wall. There were families with kids and gray-haired grandmothers. Mike and Kate even saw a Little League baseball team in uniform taking the tour. But no sign of Captain Dan.

Outside, the fog continued to roll in. Trails of mist floated past Alcatraz's old windows.

Finally, fifteen minutes before three o'clock, Mike clutched Kate's arm and pointed across the hallway. Captain Dan stood near one of the isolation cells.

Kate tugged her father's sleeve. "We'll be back in a minute," she said. "Mike wants to have another look at a cell over there."

Mike and Kate sneaked over to the far wall. As they did, Captain Dan entered the cell. They crept closer to get a better look.

Captain Dan didn't see them. He paced the room, checking his watch. Then he pulled something shiny out of his jacket pocket.

A flash of yellow and red gleamed in the dim afternoon light.

"It's Ray's World Series ring!" Mike said.

Kate stamped her foot. "We need to do something!" she said. "Otherwise, he'll sell the ring, and we won't have any proof!"

Mike rolled his tennis ball from hand to hand. "Follow me!" he said.

He stepped into the cell. "Captain Dan?" he said.

The captain plunged his hands into his pockets and spun around. When he saw Mike and Kate, he raised an eyebrow.

"Oh, hello . . . ," he said. "Funny to run into you here. Are you seeing all the San Francisco sights?"

"Kinda," Kate said. She stared at his jacket pocket.

Mike's fingers curled into his fists. He glared at Captain Dan. "Actually," Mike said, leaning forward, "we're still looking for Ray's missing ring."

Captain Dan chuckled. "Well, you're not going to find it here," he said. "I'm pretty sure it's at the bottom of the bay. It must have slipped off the old man's finger when he was treading water in McCovey Cove."

"That's what we thought, too," Kate said. "Until Mike realized that maybe it didn't. Maybe it slipped off Ray's finger and into your hand when you helped him back on the boat!"

Captain Dan glanced around nervously. "What do you mean?" he asked, looking down at the kids. "You think I took the ring? That's ridiculous. What would I do with the ring?"

Kate took a step forward. "Oh please, Captain Dan. I saw the piece of paper you left near the boat's steering wheel. It looks like you're going to sell it in about ten minutes," she said. "Why else would you write *The rock. The ring. Three pm*'?"

Captain Dan looked stunned. His eyes hardened, his forehead furrowed, and a sneer crossed his face.

"You're lucky no one can see us," he muttered under his breath. "You kids don't know what you're messing with. You need to get out of here and forget all about this. Otherwise, you might end up at the bottom of the bay, like the ring."

Without stopping, Captain Dan lunged forward.

"Look out, Kate!" Mike yelled. He grabbed Kate's arm and pulled her into the hallway.

Captain Dan snatched at empty air. He scowled, steadied himself, and then made another grab for Kate.

CLANK!

Mike slammed the heavy metal door of the prison cell shut. He jammed his tennis ball into the track to keep it closed.

BANG!

Captain Dan smashed into the cold steel of the door. The door rattled the bars of the cell, but it didn't budge.

"LET ME OUT!" Captain Dan bellowed. He pounded on the cell door. "OPEN THE DOOR!"

The other tourists in the hallway stopped to stare. Kate's dad hurried over.

"How did I know you two would be in the middle of all this noise?" he asked.

Before Mike could answer, he felt a beefy hand clamp down on his shoulder.

A blue-suited security guard turned Mike around. "You're not supposed to tamper with these cells," he said. "They're federal property!"

"But you don't understand," Mike blurted out. "We've captured a criminal! He stole a World Series ring!"

Captain Dan kept banging on the door. "LET ME OUT!" he hollered.

Another guard rapped on the cell door with a baton. "Quiet down in there," he said. "We'll let you go as soon as we figure out what's going on."

The banging stopped.

Mike and Kate explained to the guards how Ray's ring went missing the day before and how they saw Captain Dan with it.

When they finished, one of the guards went to the office to check out the story. After he returned, the guard confirmed that Ray's ring was missing. The police had emailed a photo of it.

"This is what we're looking for," he told the other guard, showing him a picture of the ring. The guards had Mike and Kate wait while they opened the cell door.

Captain Dan came out quietly. "Thanks so much, officers," he said in a cheerful voice. "We don't have to bother punishing those kids. I imagine they were only horsing around."

Captain Dan started to saunter away.

"Not so fast, buddy," the first security guard said. He twisted Captain Dan's arm behind his back. The second security guard moved the captain against the wall and started frisking him. A few seconds later, he took his hand out of Captain Dan's jacket pocket.

The guard held up the World Series ring.

The word GIANTS was stamped around the top. In the center gleamed a bright red ruby.

"I don't think you'll be going anywhere now," the guard said as they handcuffed Captain Dan and led him away.

Mike bumped Kate. "We've got to tell Ray we found his ring!" he said. "Let's go plan our *own* escape from Alcatraz!"

One More
Giant Splash

The cheers and yells were so loud, Kate, Mike, and Mr. Hopkins could hardly hear anything else.

It was Saturday night and they were sitting behind the San Francisco Giants' dugout. Ray stood on the mound. He wore an old-fashioned Giants uniform. The large video screen behind him flashed clips of his famous play against the Dodgers years ago.

"Please give a huge round of applause to Giants' all-star Ray 'the Rock' Reynolds!" the announcer said. "He was a member of one of our winning World Series teams."

Fans nearby stood and cheered. A few whistled loudly.

Ray held up his right hand with a ball clutched in it. The ball glowed white in the bright lights. But to Kate and Mike, his World Series ring stood out even more.

The crowd roared. Ray pulled himself into pitching position. His eyes stared at the plate. He planted his legs together and cradled the ball in the glove in front of his chest.

Then he drew his left leg up high and went into his windup. The fans could tell that even though he was an old-timer, Ray still had it. He fired a fastball straight over the plate.

"That's what he used to do to us," Lenny said. He was sitting next to Mike, Kate, and Mr. Hopkins. "He was a great pitcher. *Except* when

he tried those sneaky plays. I'm glad he got his ring back."

"Well, I know from some of the old coaches that you were pretty good, too," Mr. Hopkins said. "Especially when we were playing the Giants, like tonight!"

After the first inning began, Ray dropped into the empty seat next to Lenny.

"You mean I have to sit near him?" Ray groaned. He grabbed Lenny's knee and gave it a squeeze. "I guess I can put up with you. . . ."

Lenny laughed. "And I can put up with you, Ray, unless you start accusing me of stealing something else," he said. "What will it be next? Your historic baseball hat? An old batting glove?"

"Speaking of stealing, did you tell Lenny what happened to the man who took your ring?" Mr. Hopkins asked.

Ray spun his World Series ring around his finger. "The police arrested Captain Dan yesterday, thanks to Kate and Mike," he said. "They also caught the man who was going to buy the ring. He worked at the gift shop at Alcatraz. He knew a person in another country who was willing to pay a *lot* of money for it."

Mike squirmed in his seat. He was impatient to say something. "Yeah, the police called *us* last night," he said. "They told us Captain Dan confessed to everything. He had offered Ray a ride on the boat last week. He'd planned all along to find a way to steal the ring."

Lenny shook his head. "I'm glad *I* didn't go on that boat trip with you, Ray," he said. "The captain might have shoved me in the water, too! Remind me not to fly with you, either, in case the pilot has something against you."

Ray waved his hand. "Well, maybe we can

sit back and watch the game together," he said. "I don't think you'll have any trouble. Unless, of course, I'm pitching!"

Ray tossed a baseball to Lenny. Ray had signed it in bright red pen. It read *To Lenny— May the Giants Always Come Out on Top.* Ray's signature was below.

"Good to see you can still catch," Ray said. "I thought you might like it to remember today's game, since the Giants are going to win."

"I don't know about that," Lenny said. He turned the ball over in his hands. "But I know a way to make sure this doesn't help the Giants." He handed it to Kate and whispered something in her ear.

Kate tapped Mike's leg. "Come on. Lenny has a job for us. Back in a minute, Dad!"

Lenny jabbed Ray in the shoulder as Mike and Kate stood up to leave. "I finally found a

way to prove you're all wet," he said. "I'm having Kate deliver the message for me."

Mike and Kate wound their way over to the long steel railing overlooking McCovey Cove. Below them, a few kayakers bobbed in the water. Farther out floated two large sailboats.

Kate held up Ray's baseball. She waved it back and forth until one of the kayakers finally saw it. He waggled his paddle back at Kate.

Mike tugged on her sleeve. "What's going on?" he asked. "Do you know him?"

Kate shook her head. "Nope, but Lenny wanted me to take care of Ray's baseball," she said. "He thought that turning a Giants baseball into a splash hit was the right thing to do!"

Kate lofted the baseball over the railing. The ball landed with a splash just a few feet in front of the kayaker.

Within seconds, the fan had paddled over and scooped up the ball. He read the autograph on it and gave Kate and Mike a thumbs-up. Then he tucked the ball into a jacket pocket and went back to scanning for other splash hits.

Mike nodded. "Good idea!" he said. "I just wish you had waited."

"Waited for what?" Kate asked.

Mike pointed at his chest. "Waited for me to take a kayak out there before you threw it!"

BALLPARK Mysteries 7

Dugout Notes
☆ San Francisco ☆ Giants Ballpark

Candlestick Park. Before the Giants moved in 2000 to their new stadium in downtown San Francisco, they played south of the city in Candlestick Park. Candlestick Park was on the edge of the bay, and strong, cold winds made games difficult for fans and players alike. Some people say that during the 1961 All-Star Game, a pitcher was blown off the mound by the wind!

Cable cars. Cable cars run on rails in the streets. They latch on to strong steel cables that move at a steady pace under the road. The cable cars glide up and down San Francisco's many hills, stopping to let people hop on and off.

McCovey Cove. The small area of San Francisco Bay by the Giants' ballpark is called McCovey Cove in honor of Willie McCovey. It's also known as China Basin. People with nets in rafts, small boats, and kayaks flood the area on game day, hoping to capture a splash hit.

Splash dogs. Portuguese water dogs are a breed of dogs that were taught to help round up schools of fish and help fishermen retrieve broken nets. After the Giants' new ballpark opened, a special dog club sprang up. It trained Portuguese water dogs to bring back splash hits in McCovey Cove!

Alcatraz. Alcatraz Island sits in the middle of San Francisco Bay. The island was used as both a lighthouse and a military base, but most people know it as a prison. From 1934 until 1963, prisoners who caused problems at other prisons were sent to Alcatraz. No one ever escaped from

Alcatraz, except for three men who broke out and were never found. Officials think that they died trying to get across the bay.

Giant soda bottle. Above the Giants' left field is an area just for kids. It has a small baseball diamond for running and batting practice, food areas, and slides inside a giant soda bottle. Next to the soda bottle is a supersized old-fashioned baseball glove. It's modeled on a 1927 glove, so it has a space for a thumb and three fingers. Back then, many gloves had four fingers, not five!

The Willies. The Giants have had good luck with Willies. Willie Mays was one of the best all-around players. He played for the Giants in both New York and San Francisco. Willie McCovey was a great first baseman for the Giants, a fierce hitter, and a Hall-of-Famer. Some people say that he hit the longest home run ever at the Giants' old Candlestick Park.

New York Giants. The Giants moved to San Francisco from New York City the same year the Dodgers moved to Los Angeles from New York City. They became even fiercer rivals after the move. Fans love it when they play each other.

1989 earthquake. The 1989 World Series turned out to be a big rumble. Just before game three was scheduled to start, a large earthquake struck the San Francisco area. It was 7.1 on the Richter scale. No one in Candlestick Park was hurt, but there was a ten-day delay before the teams played again. Unfortunately for the Giants, the Oakland A's won in four games.